This book is to be ret...
the ...

THIS WALKER BOOK BELONGS TO:

_____

_____

_____

_____

For my granddaughter Rachel
P. L.
For Paul, with love
T. M.

First published 1994 by
Walker Books Ltd
87 Vauxhall Walk
London SE11 5HJ

This edition published 1995

2 4 6 8 10 9 7 5 3 1

Text © 1994 Penelope Lively
Illustrations © 1994 Terry Milne

The right of Penelope Lively to be identified as author of this work
has been asserted by her in accordance with the Copyright,
Designs and Patents Act 1988.

This book has been typeset in Berkeley Book.

Printed and bound in Hong Kong

British Library Cataloguing in Publication Data
A catalogue record for this book is
available from the British Library.

ISBN 0-7445-3633-2

The Cat, the Crow and the Banyan Tree

Written by PENELOPE LIVELY   Illustrated by TERRY MILNE

WALKER BOOKS
AND SUBSIDIARIES
LONDON · BOSTON · SYDNEY

The cat and the crow lived under the banyan tree.
All day long they told stories.
The cat was thin and quick and she told stories
that were elegant and entertaining.

The crow was fat and handsome and he
told stories that were fast and furious.
The banyan tree was tall and wide and
light and dark and full of secrets.

One day the cat said, "Today we're going to tell extra special stories. My turn first. Are you listening, Crow?"

"I'm listening," said the crow.

"Then I'll begin," said the cat. "There was once a crow, and a very fine fellow was he."

"I like this story," said the crow. "Go on."

And then his friend the cat, who was thin and quick and knew mysterious things, told the crow to follow her into the story and at once they found themselves in one of the hidden places of the banyan tree.

"What's this?" said the crow.
"The secret stairs," said the cat.
"Where do they go?" asked the crow.
"On and on and up and up and
round and round and into the
clouds and out the other side."
And the cat told the crow
to follow her up the
stairs, up and up
and on and on.

"I'm getting tired," the crow complained.

"A hundred and one, a hundred and two, a hundred and three…"

"Here we are!" said the cat. "Look!"

And the crow looked, and saw the sky and the stars and the great bright moon.

"Now what?" said the crow.

"Do you see the mountains of the moon?" asked the cat. "That's where we're going."

"Why?" said the crow.

"To find the end of the story," said the cat.

She called for a shooting star, and the
star pulled them through the clouds and
up into the dark sky, up and up to the
top of the highest mountain on the moon.

The crow looked around.

"So where's the end of the story?"

"Right here," said the cat. "We're at the end of the story because we climbed the stairs and found the sky and rode with the star and got to the top of the highest mountain and now we can see back to the beginning. Take the telescope and look down."

The crow looked, and far, far away he saw the banyan tree.

"There's the beginning of the story," said the cat. "Now shut your eyes and we'll go back."

When the crow
opened his eyes
he found that
they were back
underneath the
banyan tree.
"Right," said the
crow. "My turn
now. Quick!
The story's
already begun.
We're off!"

"Where to?" said the cat.
"Anywhere! Everywhere!
Look out! They're after us!"

"Who?" cried the cat.
"Everyone! Anyone!"
"Why?" gasped the cat.

"They're after our money!
Our jewels! Our gold and silver!"
"What gold? What silver?"
"It's the hullaballoos!" yelled the crow.
"Hang on tight – we'll go supersonic!"

"Ooooooh…" moaned the cat.

"We've escaped," said the crow. "Help!
Here comes the glockenspiel!"

"I don't like this story,"
wailed the cat.

"I want to
get off."

"It all works out in the
end," said the crow.
"Just you see. Whoops!
There he goes!
Now for the ghost
tunnel. Keep your
head down and sing."

"Why do
we have to
go in here?"
mewed the cat.
"To get to the other
end. Sing louder!
Scare them
off! That's
the way!…

". . . Out we come!"

"Oooooh . . . " cried the cat.
"Are we almost there?"

"Almost where?" said the
crow. "Look out! Here
comes the snake gang!
Watch your tail! Hold on tight . . .
Wheee! There we go.
Isn't this story fun?"

"I'm not sure," said the cat.
"Where's the end?"

"I think I can see it,"
said the crow. "Pass
me the telescope.
Now—going
supersonic again.
Whoosh . . . "

And there
they were
back under
the banyan tree.
"Thank goodness
for that," said the cat.
"Now what?"
said the crow.
"I'm bored."

"It's time for tea," said the cat. "And we have some visitors. I shall pour out and you may pass the cakes."

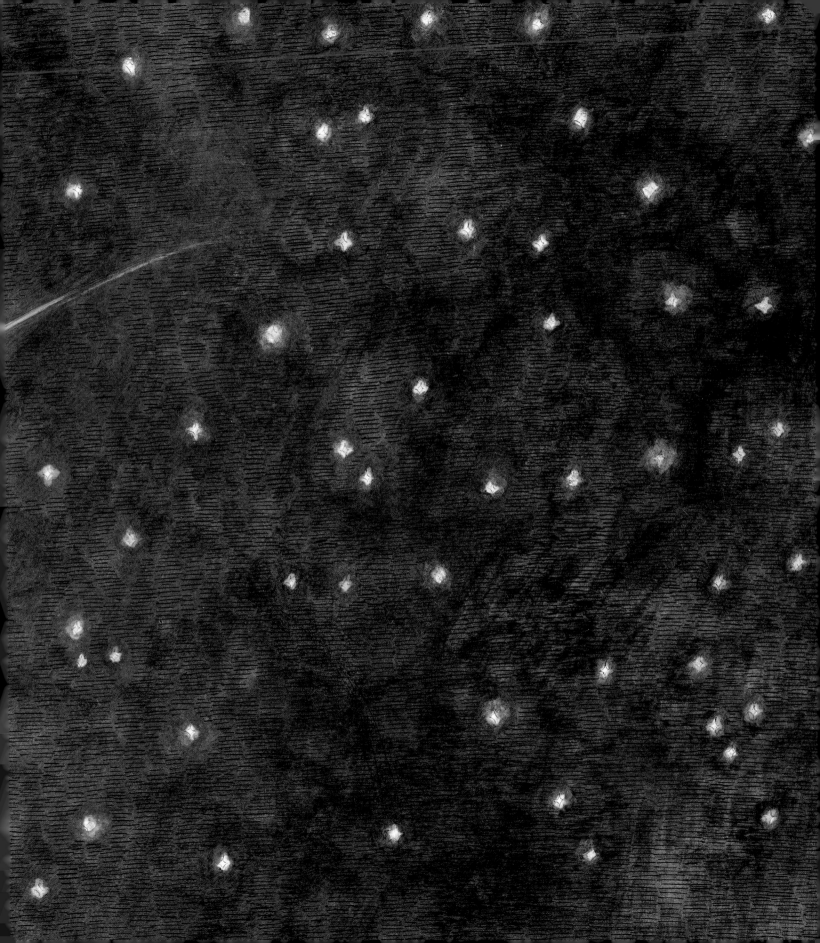

MORE WALKER PAPERBACKS
For You to Enjoy

THE TOYMAKER
by Martin Waddell/Terry Milne

A modern two-part fairy tale about youth, age and enduring love.

"Quite beautiful ... a classic. It made me cry." *BBC Radio's Treasure Islands*

0-7445-3018-0   £4.50

GRANDMA'S HAT
by Rosemary Kahn/Terry Milne

Grandma's story tells of the hat she hated and how she finally got rid of it.

"Set in 1920s colonial South Africa, Terry Milne's pencil and watercolour illustrations give us
a fascinating glimpse into the family life of white settlers and the fashions
and architecture of the period." *Books for Keeps*

0-7445-3059-8   £3.99

SOUTH AND NORTH, EAST AND WEST
The Oxfam Book of Children's Stories

edited by Michael Rosen

Animal stories from Botswana and Indonesia, ghost stories from
Jamaica and Vietnam, family stories from India and South Africa,
a creation myth from Brazil... Each of these twenty-five tales is illustrated
by an internationally acclaimed artist. All royalties benefit the work of Oxfam.

"A kaleidoscopic collection of stories from all round the world...
A great book for reading aloud, or alone." *The Guardian*

0-7445-4366-5   £7.99